BUILT MAN SELFIE

sexy

/ Sɛksi /

Learn how to pronounce

adjective

1. 1 .

sexually attractive or exciting.

"sexy French underwear"

synonyms:

sexually attractive, seductive , desirable , alluring ,
inviting , sensual , sultry , slinky , provocative , tempting ,
tantalizing ;

.

1. 2 .

INFORMAL

very exciting or appealing.

"business magazines may not seem like the sexiest
career choice"

synonyms:

exciting , stimulating , interesting , appealing , intriguing

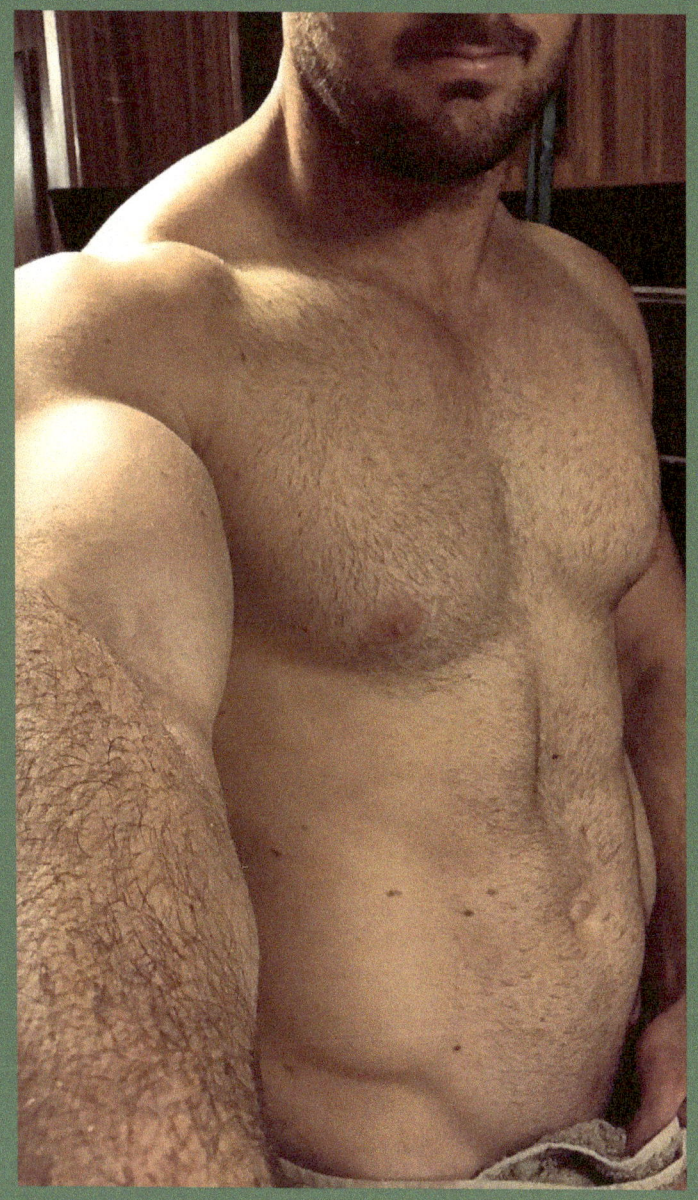

go on, flex.
YOU KNOW YOU WANT TO

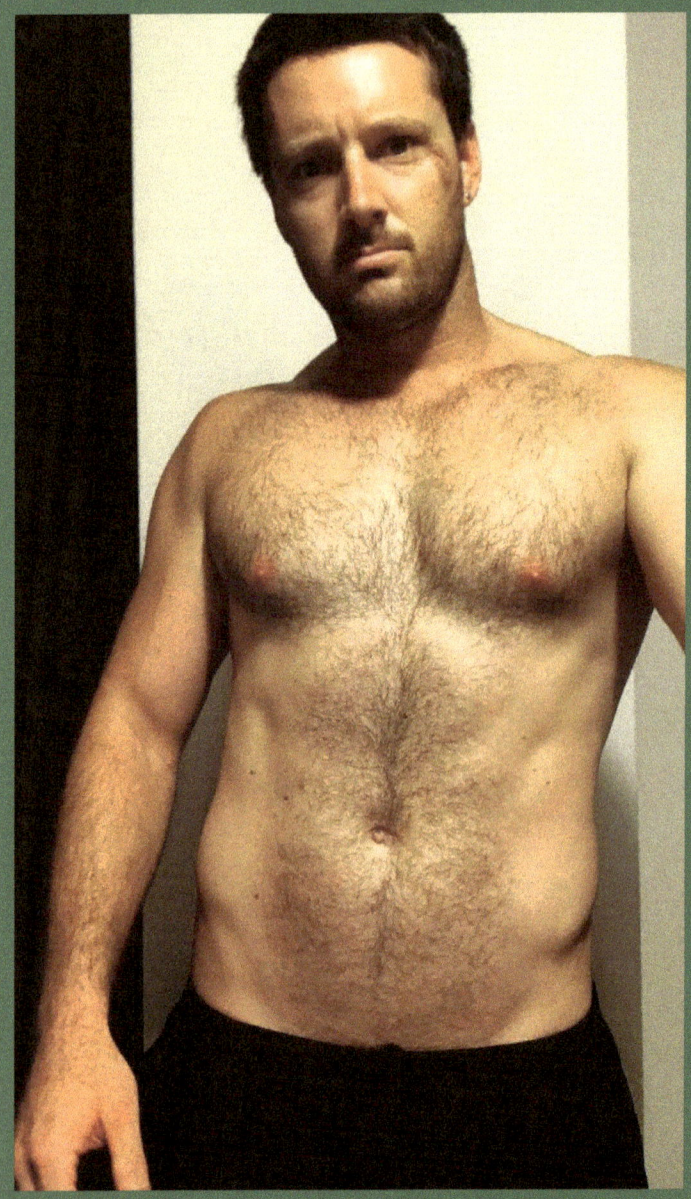

CPSIA information can be obtained
at www.ICGtesting.com
Printed in the USA
BVHW021120180719
553829BV00013B/419/P

9 780464 045380